The MAGIC SQUAD
and the Dog of
Great Potential

Mary Quattlebaum
Illustrated by Frank Remkiewicz

Delacorte Press

Acknowledgments

Thank you to Debbie Duel, director of Humane Education for the Washington Humane Society, for information and helpful insights on children and animals. Thanks, too, to Con Quattlebaum, my dad, for many childhood memories of teaching dogs to come, fetch, and stay. And my respect for their mission and my gratitude for their work also go to the American Society for the Prevention of Cruelty to Animals and other humane animal shelters and organizations.

Published by
Delacorte Press
Bantam Doubleday Dell Publishing Group, Inc.
1540 Broadway
New York, New York 10036

Library of Congress Cataloging-in-Publication Data
Quattlebaum, Mary.
The Magic Squad and the dog of great potential / Mary Quattlebaum ;
illustrated by Frank Remkiewicz.
p.   cm.
Summary: After visiting the Humane Shelter, ten-year-old Calvin wants
to help every dog there but finds it an almost impossible job.
ISBN 0-385-32276-3 (alk. paper)
[1. Dogs—Fiction.   2. Pets—Fiction.   3. Animals—Treatment—Fiction.]
I. Remkiewicz, Frank, ill.   II. Title.
PZ7.Q19Mag   1997
[Fic]—dc20   96-22216
                                                                  CIP
                                                                  AC

The text of this book is set in 13.5-point Electra.
Book design by Kimberly M. Adlerman
Manufactured in the United States of America

March 1997
10   9   8   7   6   5   4   3   2   1

To Mel, Paul, and Danny,
my three great brothers

1

CALVIN HASTINGS LAY FLAT ON HIS BACK IN ALFRED Ludlott's backyard. Calvin's city apartment building had no lawn, so today he was taking full advantage of this wide patch of tickly grass. He wiggled in deep and waggled his high-tops.

With his Walkman plugged into both ears, all Calvin could hear was music. *Hmmm, hmmm, scree-e-e,* he hummed to the jazz sound of John Coltrane's sax while the clouds above softly skated the sky.

Calvin liked to watch the world from this angle. He could see each ladybug and blade of grass. He could see the legs of the lawn table. He could see—

Calvin squinted, then groaned.

His brother Monk had done it again.

Calvin closed his eyes. Maybe he had made a mistake. He would look again.

Slowly, slowly he opened his eyes. He saw Jenny Teiteltot's red tennis shoes tucked on her chair rungs. He saw Lola Ludlott's little-girl Keds, the same bright red as Jenny's. He saw Alfred Ludlott's brown, scuffed shoes and his brother Monk's old, gray-white Nikes. . . .

Calvin sighed. Yeah, Monk had done it again.

Draped around his brother's right ankle was one sloppy white sock. Rising smoothly above the left was another sock—blue. Not light blue or powder blue, but *electric* blue, a shocking hue, screamingly different from white.

Lying in tickly grass, staring at his brother's odd socks, Calvin sighed again. Wouldn't you think a guy eight years old would *finally* have learned how to dress?

Most kids, yes. But not Monk.

Monk wore summer shorts with winter sweaters; he wore mismatched, untied shoes. Why, just this morning, Calvin had had to snatch his brother by the collar of his inside-out T-shirt—and help to fix it right side in.

Did Monk ever look in a mirror? Calvin wondered, and knew the answer: No. Monk was too busy looking into books of every shape and size. He was too busy reading big print and small print and poems of every kind: short, long, silly, sad, rhymed, and unrhymed. Monk liked to write poems, too, and read them aloud.

Poems, Calvin thought. Why *poems?* Maybe there was some gene Monk had inherited that made him love to mess around with words the way other kids liked to play with trucks, say, or trains or dolls.

Last year, Calvin would have sworn that Monk was a kook.

Now he knew differently.

"Kook" was not the right word anymore. His brother Monk was a TAG.

Talented and Gifted. T-A-G.

In fact, this year Monk was enrolled in a special class for brainy kids. This class would provide "enriching" experiences, according to Dad and Mom. As far as Calvin could tell, this meant the TAG kids were going to see plays and visit the houses of dead, famous folks. They were expected to do extra schoolwork.

Extra schoolwork, thought Calvin. Poor Monk. But his brother was actually excited. Second grade had been boring, he had told Calvin. Maybe this third-grade TAG stuff would be better.

And now Monk's being a TAG was the reason why Calvin was stretched out in the green, green, tickly grass of Alfred Ludlott, the poet.

Usually after school, Calvin, Monk, and their neighbor Jenny Teiteltot stayed with Ms. Eva in their city apartment building until their parents got home from work. But for the first six weeks of this school year, Ms. Eva was touring the East Coast with her group of older jazz dancers, the Silver Threads. Calvin did not see why Ms. Eva's absence should present a problem. He offered to be the after-school sitter—and at *half* of Ms. Eva's pay.

"No," Dad and Mom had said together. "Ten years old is too young."

Then Alfred Ludlott had called. He was a poet and retired professor who sometimes visited Monk's school. His granddaughter, Lola, thought Jenny was *wonderful*. Alfred wanted to invite the Hastings and Jenny to a poetry reading, and when he learned they needed an after-school sitter— well, he promptly offered his help. This was the plan: Each day after school for six weeks Calvin, Jenny, and Monk would ride their bus until it reached Alfred Ludlott's house. The poet would be their sitter.

Calvin did not think this was a very good plan. Alfred Ludlott often seemed as fog-brained as Monk. He reminded Calvin of a bewildered bird. Personally, Calvin thought Alfred Ludlott had enough to do just watching four-year-old Lola, who was as bright-eyed and quick as a hamster. Maybe Alfred Ludlott wanted *them* to watch Lola. Calvin shuddered at the thought.

Monk, that poem-loving TAG, was thrilled with this after-school plan. Jenny was happy as long as she could practice her magic. In Calvin's opinion, Jenny was as obsessed with magic as Monk was with poetry. Just listening to them, Calvin figured he had learned more about poetry and magic than any non-poet, non-magician in the world. And now his after-school hours would be spent with a grown-up poet and his tiny granddaughter, who copied everything Jenny did, *especially* magic.

Six weeks of *twice* the usual talk about poetry and magic. And Calvin couldn't even bring along his hamster, Pizzazz. The long, noisy bus rides would frighten him (and Jenny's guinea pig, Blackstone). At least Alfred Ludlott had a dog. Maybe this dog would keep Calvin from missing Pizzazz so much.

And Dad's present made Calvin feel better, too. Dad had given him a Walkman.

"This way," Dad explained, showing Calvin how to work the new earphones, "you can listen to your music without, uh, disturbing anyone. Alfred Ludlott needs to write, you know."

Frowning, Calvin had pulled out one earphone. "What do you mean, 'disturb'? Coltrane's music does not *disturb* anyone."

"Well," said Dad, "there *are* a lot of squeaks and bleats and snorts."

"Those are *notes*," said Calvin.

"Sometimes," Dad said, "those notes sound like noise—but maybe I don't know how to listen."

That was what Calvin thought, too. His father did not know how to listen. Calvin loved the way John Coltrane could make his notes tumble down, a wash of sound, like clean rain rinsing the sky. When Ms. Eva and the Silver Threads played their jazz tapes, Calvin could feel the music filling his mind and body, starting his high-tops to movin'.

"When you snore," Calvin said, "I don't consider it noise. I *like* your bleats and snorts."

Dad looked surprised. "Do I snore?"

Calvin nodded. "Loudly," he said.

"Well, anyway." Dad quickly shifted the talk away from music and snores. "Homework. You can do your homework each day at Alfred Ludlott's house. It will be quiet there."

Dad hesitated, then added, "Calvin, I think if you studied harder, focused more on your homework, you could do better this year. You have a lot of potential."

Calvin had nodded, but inside he thought, Homework? Who worried about homework the first week of school?

Why was his father so pushy about homework all of a sudden? Wasn't it enough to have one TAG son? Did he want Calvin to be a TAG, too?

Now, listening to his Walkman in Alfred Ludlott's yard, Calvin let all thoughts of homework ease out of his brain. He really liked this song "Chasin' the Trane." It was full of big sounds, wonderful sounds, like the chuffing rush of a locomotive, like his dad's loud snores from his chair. Calvin turned his head away from his brother's odd socks and contemplated the rest of the yard. He saw upside-down stems, the splash of pansies, a few leaves drifting to earth. He watched four stubby legs waddle past.

Fitzgerald, Alfred Ludlott's elderly dachshund, didn't even pause for a friendly pat. He wiggled his long sausage body though his small doggy door and disappeared. As a dog, Fitzgerald sure was a disappointment, Calvin thought. He didn't chase Frisbees and wouldn't fetch sticks. Fitzgerald seemed happy mostly to sleep.

"Calvin!"

Calvin felt one earphone get yanked from his ear.

"Calvin!"

"What?" He turned his head and bumped his nose on Jenny's red sneaker.

"Don't step on me," he shouted.

Two red sneakers took one step back.

Jenny sniffed. "Your dad's ready to take us home."

Lola sniffed, too. Her tiny red sneakers took one step back.

Calvin jumped to his feet and dusted the seat of his pants.

"So how was life at Alfred Ludlott's today?" Dad asked as they walked to the car.

"I wrote a new poem," said Monk, "and finished my homework."

"Wonderful," said Dad. "This TAG program isn't too much work for you, is it?"

"I like it," said Monk.

"Good, good." Dad nodded.

"I started my six-week project," said Jenny. "We have to pick a topic—whatever we want—and do lots of research and give a report to the class. We can draw pictures or use photos or do an experiment—anything to make it interesting."

Calvin scuffed his toe on the grass. Geez! Why was Jenny chatting about their six-week project already? It was only the first week of school.

Jenny took a breath before rushing on. "Do you want to hear my topic? I'm going to do my project on—"

"Magic." Calvin sighed.

Jenny beamed. "Yes! How did you know?"

Up to this point—fifth grade—Jenny had done every project, every report, every kindergarten show-and-tell on magic. Calvin figured this year would be no different. Fabulous props, amazing card tricks, the life and death of Harry Houdini—Jenny never ran out of ideas.

Dad smiled. "Magic sounds interesting." He

picked a grass blade from Calvin's T-shirt. "And what did you do this afternoon, son?"

"I thought about my project, too," Calvin said loudly. Which was true. Hadn't he been forced to think about it as soon as Jenny had mentioned hers?

"You did?" Dad looked surprised, then pleased. "That's great! You're planning ahead."

"Planning ahead," Calvin repeated.

Actually, he did not like to plan ahead. It caused too much worry. Calvin was a C kind of guy. C in math; C in English; C for Calvin, straight-C guy. Sometimes it was hard to be around such a plan-ahead kid as Jenny or such a supersmart one as Monk. Their work was bound to make his own look, well, kind of measly.

Dad clapped a hand to Monk's shoulder, a hand to Calvin's. "Sounds like this year is off to a good start for everyone."

Jenny raised one skeptical eyebrow at Calvin.

So did Lola.

Calvin looked down at his grass-stained high-tops. Well, he *was* thinking about his project. Really he was. Even if he was thinking about how much he didn't want to think about it. Besides, he had *plenty* of time.

THE FIRST WEEK OF SCHOOL HAD GONE BY AS SLOWLY as school usually does, bringing nothing but more and harder work and a C– on a quiz Calvin had really meant to study for. Monk, of course, had brought home several gold stars, smiley faces, "Excellent!"s, and As. Oh well, Calvin thought, lying in his favorite flat-back position in Alfred Ludlott's yard. Nothing I can do about that. He lazily watched as Jenny shuffled a deck of cards.

"Pick a card, any card," Jenny singsonged to Monk, who had his nose in a book.

"Pick a card," Lola echoed.

Without lifting his eyes from the page, Monk lifted one card from the fanned deck, looked, and stuck it back.

Then Jenny put on a great card-shuffling show.

She snapped and cracked that deck. She made fans and cascades. And she didn't drop a single card.

Calvin was amazed. He remembered a time when Jenny's tricks had been more mess-up than magic. Wands broke, scarves dropped, coins rolled all over the floor. Calvin had to admit Jenny had gotten better . . . much better.

Jenny pulled one card from the deck. "My dear sir," she said to Monk in her best magician voice. "My dear sir, take a look, a long, long look, at this card"—she paused dramatically—"and tell me, is this the card—the exact same card—you had picked before?"

"Abracadab! Abracadab!" cried Lola.

Monk did not look up.

"My dear sir," Jenny started again. "Is this—"

Lola bonked Monk's head.

"Ow!" Monk looked up. "Why'd you do that?"

"Monk-is-this-the-card-the-very-same-card?" Jenny singsonged rapidly before Monk could dive back into his book.

Monk rubbed his head. He squinted at the card. He straightened his glasses, squinted again.

"Ah," he said slowly, still squinting. "You know, Jenny, I . . . forget."

Jenny snorted in disgust. "That's pitiful! How can I practice for my class project if no one will give me the least—the teeniest—bit of help?"

"Class project." Those words again. Calvin closed his eyes. Why did Jenny have to start her project early? She started every project early. She'd been starting projects early since first grade.

What a waste of time, Calvin thought. What a lot of worry.

"Hey, you guys!"

Calvin heard a holler from the other side of the fence. He opened his eyes and waved.

Dr. Jamar, the veterinarian, waved back.

Calvin liked Dr. Jamar. She was calm and friendly. Although she lived in Alfred Ludlott's neighborhood, her office was close to Calvin's apartment building. Calvin sometimes liked to visit the sick dogs and cats in her clean waiting room. Once she had even treated his hamster, Pizzazz.

"Where are you going?" he asked.

"To the humane shelter," Dr. Jamar replied.

"Who's Hugh Main?" Calvin asked.

"Not who, *what*," said Dr. Jamar. "The humane shelter helps homeless animals."

Now Calvin really got interested. He liked animals. In fact, Pizzazz was one of his best buddies. So was Blackstone, Jenny's white guinea pig, who had been named for two famous magicians, a father and son.

Suddenly there was a high-pitched yip, and a brown blur raced through the yard.

Calvin had never seen Fitzgerald move so fast. The old dog greeted Dr. Jamar with tail wags that shook his whole stubby body.

Well, Calvin thought sadly, here was an animal who was not his friend. Not that he, Calvin, hadn't tried to be friendly. It was just that Fitzgerald usually wanted to sleep.

"Hey, can I go to the humane shelter with you?" he asked.

Dr. Jamar looked surprised. "I—"

"Thanks! Let me tell Alfred Ludlott," hollered Calvin, running into the house.

In seconds he was back, beaming beside the still-surprised Dr. Jamar.

"Why do you want to go to the humane shelter?" Jenny asked, shuffling her cards.

"Because." Calvin paused.

Jenny lifted one skeptical eyebrow.

"Because," said Calvin boldly, "because I've never been before. It's *enriching.*"

Even Lola snorted, but Calvin chose to ignore the rude sounds as he jumped into Dr. Jamar's car. He felt a bit like a TAG kid going on a special—an *enriching*—educational trip.

"I'm going to pick up a little dog—" Dr. Jamar began.

"A puppy!" Calvin exclaimed.

Dr. Jamar shook her head. "Actually, Biscuit is about five years old. She once belonged to someone else."

"You want a *used* dog?" Calvin asked.

Dr. Jamar smiled. "I'm going to foster Biscuit for about one month, which means she will live with me until I find her a new home."

"I don't think," said Calvin, "many people will want a *used* dog when they can buy a *new* puppy."

"Calvin," said Dr. Jamar sadly, "I'm afraid you're right."

When the car pulled into the humane shelter, Calvin heard the dogs even before he saw them.

The air was filled with yips, barks, yaps, and howls.

Calvin saw rows of wire pens with clean concrete

floors. Each pen contained a house and bowls for water and food.

Each pen contained a dog.

Most of the dogs barked and paced. Some scratched their doors and yapped. A few peered silently from doghouses.

There were dogs of all shapes, colors, and sizes. German shepherds, collies, poodles, and mutts. Very few were puppies.

"Dr. Jamar," said Calvin, stunned, "why are there so many dogs?"

"All these dogs need homes," said Dr. Jamar. "In fact, every year in shelters across the country, there are millions of dogs and cats that need homes."

"Why?" cried Calvin.

Dr. Jamar shrugged. "Sometimes owners move away or can't take care of their pets, so they bring their dogs and cats here. Or the animals grow out of the cute baby stage—and become nuisances. They chew the furniture or jump on guests, and the owners don't take the time to train them properly." She hesitated, then said, "Sometimes people hurt their pets. To protect the animals, the staff of the humane shelter will take them away."

As she spoke, Dr. Jamar moved closer to one pen, knelt down, and began talking softly to the small dog inside.

"Come, Biscuit," she called. "Come."

The dog—whose coat, indeed, was the color of biscuits—gazed with dark eyes at the kneeling woman, then suddenly—*plunk!*—flattened herself to the floor.

She looked like a pancake with a little dog head.

"Is that a trick?" Calvin asked, amazed.

Dr. Jamar continued to call gently until Biscuit rose and came, trembling, to be patted through the wire.

Finally Dr. Jamar answered Calvin's question. "Biscuit is afraid." The veterinarian stroked the dog's ears. "She is confused. Her whole world has turned upside down. Her owner, the person she lived with and trusted, recently died—"

"Died?" asked Calvin.

Dr. Jamar nodded. "Her owner was very old, but Biscuit doesn't know that. She only knows that her owner has disappeared, that suddenly she is in this strange place, with strange dogs and noises and smells. Strange people look at her, pat her, and go away." Dr. Jamar took a deep breath. "If what happened to Biscuit happened to me . . . well, I think I'd want to go flat-frightened, too."

Calvin nodded. He looked around at the other dogs and wondered why they were here.

And that was when he noticed one particular dog.

With one brown ear up and one spotted ear down, the dog regarded Calvin with bright, brown eyes. His skinny tail wagged furiously.

"Hey, dog," said Calvin.

"Roo-roo," answered the dog. His bark was loud and cheerful. His tail wagged faster.

"Roo-roo-roo," he saluted Calvin again.

"Dr. Jamar!" Calvin called. "Here's a great dog to foster!"

Dr. Jamar snapped a leash to Biscuit's collar and looked at the huge, roo-rooing creature.

"I'm afraid," she sighed, "that dog doesn't have a very good chance of finding a new home. He's so big, and I don't think he's been trained." She glanced at the small dog beside her. "Biscuit," she said, "heel."

Biscuit hesitated, then stepped out, close to Dr. Jamar's left leg. Calvin fell into step beside them.

"But that dog is *smart*," Calvin argued. "He has

great potential, you can tell from his eyes. Anyone could train him."

"Training takes a lot of time and patience," said Dr. Jamar. "I've seen some carelessly trained dogs, and, believe me, their behavior was weird."

"So he has to stay *here*?" Calvin asked indignantly. "Maybe for years?"

Dr. Jamar hesitated. "Calvin," she said gently, "if a dog isn't adopted in about one week, he is . . . he is put to sleep."

Calvin knew what that meant. "Put to sleep" meant the dog would die.

"Why?" he cried.

"They have to make room for other dogs that need homes—"

"Why don't they let him go?" Calvin interrupted.

"That would be cruel," said Dr. Jamar. "Where would he go? He might get hit by a car. He might starve or get sick. At the humane shelter, he is cared for and he has a chance . . ."

Calvin could only shake his head.

When they reached the car, Dr. Jamar tucked Biscuit into the backseat. The little dog curled up quietly.

Calvin looked back at the humane shelter.

"Roo-roo-roo," he heard the big dog call above all the other barks.

"Dr. Jamar." Calvin shook his head harder. "Dr. Jamar."

"I know, Calvin," she said. She touched his shoulder gently. "Sometimes I feel sad, too, when I come here."

They sat together in the car, listening to Biscuit's breathing and to the muffled barking of dogs.

"But feeling sad does not help those animals." Dr. Jamar started the car. "Feeling sad changes nothing."

Calvin wiped his eyes with the back of his hand.

"There's so much that *can* be done," Dr. Jamar continued, as if to herself. "Fostering, volunteering, fund-raising—oh, I'm sorry, Calvin," she said. "I can go on and on."

"That's okay," said Calvin quietly. The car hummed through the city traffic. Finally he broke the silence. "Do you ever, you know, want to keep a dog you've fostered?"

"Sometimes," said Dr. Jamar, "but it seems more important to find that one dog a good home and use my place as a foster home for others."

"How many dogs have you fostered?" Calvin asked.

"About fifty."

Calvin thought about the millions of dogs that needed homes.

"Fifty," he said, "is not a lot."

"It's something," said Dr. Jamar. "It's something I can do."

Calvin thought about Dr. Jamar's big yard, the money she had to buy dog food. "But I'm a kid," he said. "What can kids do? I mean, *really* do?"

Dr. Jamar sailed smoothly past a big truck. "You'd be surprised," she said, "at what kids can do."

FRIDAY. THE END OF THE SECOND SCHOOL WEEK. The sun was warm, the grass smelled sweet, but Calvin barely noticed. Lying flat on his back, he was thinking about that dog at the shelter. That big, glad-barking dog.

Dr. Jamar had told him that kids could do a lot to help animals. Calvin could donate old towels and money to the humane shelter. He could write letters about adopting pets from shelters and send them to newspapers and kids' magazines. He could report cruel treatment of pets. Those actions, Dr. Jamar had told him, could help many dogs and cats.

Calvin knew that was important.

But he wanted especially to help one dog. One particular dog.

And towels, money, and letters would not help that dog.

That dog needed a home.

Calvin knew he could not give that dog a home. His apartment building did not allow dogs or cats; and, anyway, this big dog needed a big space. Even Pizzazz's hamster cage, small as it was, sometimes crowded his family's place.

At moments like this, Calvin especially missed Pizzazz. He felt he could think more clearly with his hamster buddy cupped in his palm.

Calvin knew he could not give the dog a home.

But *maybe* he could convince someone else to give the dog a home.

Calvin sighed. Dr. Jamar had already said no. "I'm sorry, Calvin"—she had shaken her head—"but I wouldn't have the time to train him. And I don't think anyone would give a home to a large, untrained dog. When the foster time ended, he'd just have to return to the shelter."

So the question remained: How to rescue the large dog? Calvin mulled over a few schemes. Maybe the dog could save a drowning child, for example, or bite a robber, and the grateful family would clasp him forever in their arms.

But even in Calvin's best daydreams, the little details didn't quite work. . . .

From his flat-back thinking position, Calvin could see Fitzgerald's white muzzle on Alfred Ludlott's brown shoe. He heard the *scratch-scratch* of the poet's pen. He heard the other kids talking to Lola's mother on the porch.

Crinkle, crinkle—the sound of Alfred Ludlott balling up his paper.

Calvin had never met a person who worked so hard and wrote so few words. Like Monk, Alfred Ludlott wanted every single sound to be perfect. The man needed to re*lax*, Calvin decided. He needed to stretch out in his big yard.

His big yard.

Alfred Ludlott had a yard. A big, big yard.

Calvin sat up. "Excuse me," he called.

Scratch, scratch, went the poet's pen.

"Ex-cuuuse me," Calvin called more loudly.

The poet looked up. "Oh, Calvin, aahhh, sorry, hmmm," he murmured.

Calvin recognized that dazed, faraway expression. It often settled on his brother's face when Monk was reading or writing.

Calvin knew he had to get through before the poet dove back to his scratching.

"Sir!" He emphasized the word "sir." "How would you like to make a difference?"

"Hmmm." The poet ran a hand through his wispy hair.

"A *big* difference," Calvin persisted.

"Calvin!" The poet sat bolt upright, rolling the dachshund off his shoe. "That's *exactly* what I was writing about. The need for each person to make a difference."

Calvin blinked. Fitzgerald glared.

"*Everyone* should give something good to the world."

"Really?" asked Calvin. He began to feel rather hopeful.

"Yes, yes, yes," said the poet, all fired up.

Calvin caught some of the poet's fired-up spirit. "This one thing you can do," he said, "is very, very good. It will mean the difference between life . . . and death."

The poet nodded.

"It involves . . ." Calvin swallowed. "This life-and-death matter involves . . ."

"Yes, yes," said the poet.

"A dog."

"A dog?" Alfred Ludlott looked disappointed. "I already have a dog."

Fitzgerald kept glaring at Calvin.

"Not just *a* dog," said Calvin. "One particular dog. At the humane shelter." He felt the burst of hope ebbing away, but he rushed on. "This dog has great potential. Dr. Jamar even thinks so."

"Then why doesn't Dr. Jamar help?"

"She's already fostering one dog," said Calvin, "and she can't take care of another." He decided to leave out the part about the dog's large size and lack of training. "See, *sir*, you don't have to keep this dog forever. You just *foster* him for one month until you find him a new owner. Only one month, and you will make a big—a *huge*—difference."

Alfred Ludlott looked very bewildered. "Oh, I don't know," he said. "I don't have a place—"

"You have this huge yard!"

"Fitzgerald might not like—"

"This dog will be *company* for Fitzgerald."

Alfred Ludlott rubbed both hands over his wispy hair. "I don't think—"

"But he'll die!" cried Calvin.

"I'm sorry." The poet slumped in his chair.

Calvin felt his last bit of hope dwindle away.

"Calvin," repeated the poet. "I'm sorry—"

"But sorry doesn't help that dog," said Calvin. "Excuse me, but now I have to think of some way that will *really* help. I don't want him to die."

Calvin slumped down on the grass, just missing the dachshund.

A strange expression crossed Alfred Ludlott's face.

"Calvin," he said slowly, "I'm ashamed of myself. I was being a hypocrite."

Did grown-ups feel ashamed? Calvin wondered, rolling up again. Usually they seemed to believe that shame belonged to kids. This was the first time Calvin had ever heard of a grown person feeling that way.

Without a doubt, Alfred Ludlott was the strangest grown-up Calvin had ever known.

"A hypocrite?" he asked.

Alfred Ludlott nodded. "I was all talk about wanting to make a difference," he said, "without doing anything."

"So"—Calvin eyed the poet—"you *do* want to make a difference."

"Yes," said Alfred Ludlott, "but you have to make a difference, too."

"Yeah?"

"Yeah. If I foster this dog, *you* have to find him a home. In one month."

"That's easy," said Calvin confidently. "Anyone setting eyes on this dog—anyone even taking the tiniest *peek*—will surely want to adopt him. Maybe you'll want to keep—"

"No," said Alfred Ludlott firmly. "That is *not* our agreement."

"Okay, okay," said Calvin cheerfully. "But you'll see how easy it is to make a difference."

Later Calvin repeated that sentence, but this time a bit anxiously. He and Alfred Ludlott were staring into the humane shelter pen at the large, loud-barking dog. The dog was chasing the tip of his own skinny tail. "See," said Calvin. "We can make a *big* difference."

"Well," said Alfred Ludlott, "he is certainly a *big* dog."

"Roo-roo-roo!" The dog whisked round and round after his tail.

"He is very intelligent," said Calvin loudly. "Look at his eyes!"

"Hmmm," said Alfred Ludlott.

"He has *great* potential."

"Indeed," said the poet.

Calvin felt his hopeful spirit go flat. It felt as flat as Biscuit, the worried pancake dog. Calvin knew that when grown-ups said "indeed" in that particular way, they usually meant "no."

"Well." Alfred Ludlott sighed. "Let's get this pup on a leash and head for home. I said I would try to make a difference, and I will—a *big* difference."

Calvin was so happy he ignored the poet's worried emphasis on the word "big." Without a doubt, Alfred Ludlott was the strangest grown-up Calvin had ever known. You never knew how his mind might work, Calvin decided. Maybe it had something to do with being a poet.

But Calvin wasn't complaining.

As Alfred Ludlott signed his name to some papers, the humane shelter officer explained that the big dog was a mixed breed. "This dog is a little of everything," said the man, counting on his fingers. "German shepherd, terrier, hound, pointer."

"A mutt," murmured Alfred Ludlott.

The man grinned. "A bargain," he said. "You get four dogs in one. Just think, sir: Each breed performs a certain kind of work. German shepherds guard, terriers dig, hounds hunt, and pointers point. No telling what this dog might do!"

"Really?" Calvin cast a look of respect at the dog.

"Really?" Alfred Ludlott cast a look of dismay.

"This dog," promised the officer, "has great potential."

Calvin beamed as he took the leash.

"Be careful there," said the man. "That dog's name is Train because—"

Whomp! went the leash as the big dog surged forward.

"*Aargh!*" went Calvin. His right arm felt wrenched from its socket. He gripped the leash more tightly. "Easy, boy! Easy!" he panted.

Finally the big dog sat down. His long pink tongue rolled out and he grinned a big dog grin.

Calvin rubbed one leash-sore hand and patted the dog with the other. This dog was BIG, a rush of power. This dog was like Calvin's favorite Coltrane song, the one called "Chasin' the Trane."

Calvin grinned. "Train" was the perfect name.

"Calvin," said Alfred Ludlott grimly, "you didn't tell me that this dog wasn't trained."

"A minor detail," said Calvin. The grin left his face.

"I don't see how—"

"*I'll* train him," Calvin broke in.

"*You'll* train him?" Alfred Ludlott looked helplessly at the humane shelter officer, who shrugged.

"It's worth a try," said the man. "Otherwise, we'll have to put him to sleep."

"See!" cried Calvin.

"Roo-roo-roo," barked the dog, as if in protest.

"He can already guard, dig, hunt, and point," Calvin said. "How hard will it be to teach him to come, sit, and heel?"

"One month," said Alfred Ludlott, whose expression had grown more dismayed. "You have one month to find this dog a new home."

One month, thought Calvin, is a long time. A lot can happen in one month.

The dog lunged forward like a locomotive. Calvin's right arm strained.

"Chasin' the Trane" hummed through his head. Chasing the Train.

On Monday, Calvin did not occupy his favorite lying-down spot in Alfred Ludlott's backyard.

Jenny, and Monk (in mismatched socks), sat at the lawn table surrounded by books.

And Calvin sat there, too. In front of him was a big stack of books.

Books on training dogs.

Over the weekend, Dad had taken them to the library. Of course, Monk had checked out poetry books for his TAG class. Of course, Jenny had checked out magic books for her project. Of course, Dad had turned to Calvin and said a few words—a few words that made Calvin squirm: "So, Calvin, what's the topic of your project?" "Umm, er" had been Calvin's reply. Then, amazingly enough, Dad had glanced at Calvin's library books, smiled, and said, "Let me guess. Your big project is . . ." Calvin waited with bated breath. "Your big project is . . . on dogs!" Calvin had looked down at his stack. "Er," he had said again. "Er, yes. Dogs. Exactly."

But a project on dogs was a good idea, Calvin decided, leaving the library. He could do a poster on different dog breeds. He could write down the ways that kids could help homeless animals. They could donate old towels and money to shelters, Calvin thought, and adopt older dogs rather than buying puppies. Calvin thought and thought about his project until he felt he had almost finished it. It would be great—and easy, too. He still had plenty of time.

Now, at Alfred Ludlott's lawn table, Calvin again read the titles of his books: *Three Weeks to a Better-Behaved Dog*; *Fast Track to a Well-Mannered Pooch*; and *Developing Your Dog's Potential*.

The books were very thick. There were many photos of well-behaved dogs and smiling trainers.

Calvin felt supremely confident. After all, how hard could it be to train Train, a dog with the talents of four dog breeds?

So what if Train's recent behavior in Alfred Ludlott's car had not been . . . very smart? Such behavior surely would never occur again.

The behavior had begun the moment they left the humane shelter. It continued all the way to Alfred Ludlott's home.

"Roo-roo-roo!" Train had sat in the backseat of Alfred Ludlott's car like a royal pet in a king's coach. And he had barked and barked and *barked*.

He barked at every single dog he saw. He barked at dogs in cars, dogs in houses, dogs on leashes and sidewalks.

"Hey," said Calvin, "I never knew the city had so many dogs."

"*Please* keep that dog quiet." Alfred Ludlott clutched the steering wheel. "I can't concentrate!"

Calvin tried, but he did not succeed. Train continued to roo-roo-roo at every single dog they passed.

"I think," Calvin tried to explain, "that Train is *guarding* you. His German shepherd genes are coming out."

Alfred Ludlott did not answer.

"Roo-roo-roo," said Train.

* * *

But Calvin figured all that out-of-control barking was in the past. Now Train was tied up in Alfred Ludlott's backyard. He was the proud owner of a new doghouse and new bowls for water and food.

He was quietly, happily digging a hole.

Calvin opened one of the dog-training books. He read the first lesson on teaching a dog to come, and his confidence soared. This was easy! Why, in no time, he and a well-behaved Train would be posing for a dog-book photo.

"Roo-roo-roo," Train barked.

Calvin looked up. That Train was one great watchdog! He had warned Calvin that Alfred and Lola Ludlott were approaching.

Alfred Ludlott did not look pleased at Train's great watchdog bark. In fact, he clapped his hands to his ears.

"Want to hear my poem?" Monk waved a piece of paper.

"Er," said Calvin and Jenny at the same time that Alfred Ludlott said, "Yes!"

"It's a limerick," said Monk. "A limerick is a funny poem, so it's okay to laugh." He proceeded to read:

There once was a large dog named Train
Who was digging a hole in the plain.
His bark was a roar
And our ears grew quite sore
From the talk of that Train on a rein.

Everyone laughed and clapped.

Except Calvin.

That poem seemed kind of insulting. Why hadn't his brother focused on Train's many fine points? The dog's friendliness, for example, or his handsome, lopsided ears. And Monk had gotten some important facts wrong. "Train is *not* digging in a plain," Calvin pointed out. "He is *not* on a rein."

"But those words rhyme," Monk explained.

"Also," Calvin continued, "Train does not *roar*, he *roos*. You shouldn't change the facts."

"Poetic license," murmured Monk, again happily scratching away.

What a TAG, Calvin thought, noticing his brother's untied shoes, the laces trailing like tired worms. "Is that your homework?" he asked.

Monk straightened his glasses and gave his

dreamy smile. "My homework? Oh, that's finished. It was pretty easy today. This is just extra—for fun."

Homework—easy? Calvin never found homework easy or fun. More like hard and boring. How had his parents' genes gotten so mixed up, Calvin wondered, to make Monk so smart and him a C kind of guy?

"Grandpa!" Lola's whisper, almost as loud as Train's roo, cut into his thoughts. "Grandpa, tell Jenny, you know . . ."

"Oh, right." Alfred Ludlott turned to Jenny. "Lola is having a birthday soon. She'll be five years old, and she wants a magician at her party."

"Good idea." Jenny nodded. "Who's the magician?"

"You!" yelled Lola.

"If you want the job," said Alfred Ludlott. "I can offer fifty dollars."

"Fif-ty dol-lars." Jenny's mouth dropped.

"That's what I would pay any other magician," said Alfred Ludlott.

"Fif-ty," Jenny repeated. "Yes, I'll be the magician!"

"Thank you, Jenny. You'll do a great job," said Alfred Ludlott before turning back to the house. "By the way, Calvin, could I have a word with you inside?"

"Sure," said Calvin, closing his book. What could Alfred Ludlott want? He had just praised Jenny's magic. Maybe the poet was going to praise Calvin's dog training! Calvin got ready for a compliment.

Alfred Ludlott handed him a brown paper bag. Inside were seven brown lumps.

"Those are bulbs," said Alfred Ludlott. "They turn into flowers. Tulips, to be exact."

Seven ugly bulbs rattled in the bag.

"They *were* in the ground," said the poet.

Calvin peered at the bulbs.

"*Were* in the ground," the poet repeated.

Suddenly Calvin's mind filled with a picture—a picture of Train digging a hole.

"I guess"—Calvin swallowed—"Train's terrier genes are coming out."

"Yes." Alfred Ludlott closed the bag. "And you need to make sure his terrier genes stop at that one hole. I can't have a destructive dog in my yard. Do you understand?"

Calvin nodded. He slowly returned to the lawn table, climbed onto the bench, and opened a dog-training book.

From the corner of his eye, he could see Train, front paws working, busy enlarging his hole.

LUCKILY FOR CALVIN, TRAIN DUG NO MORE HOLES. The dog merely concentrated on deepening the one he had started. And Calvin concentrated on teaching Train to come.

He worked with Train on Tuesday, Wednesday, and Thursday. He followed the directions in the dog-training books.

Calvin was not successful.

He was even less successful at teaching Train to be quiet.

"Roo-roo-roo," Train hollered whenever Fitzgerald plunked through his doggy door and waddled across the yard.

"Quiet, *quiet*," Calvin would holler, stroking the big dog's head.

"Roo-roo-roo," Train would respond, as loudly as ever.

On Friday, Fitzgerald sauntered back and forth four times. He's teasing Train, Calvin thought indignantly. He was glad Monk was on a TAG trip. He wanted no more limericks about Train's vigorous bark.

Dad had gone on the TAG trip, too, Calvin remembered. Dad had been very excited. He had asked Monk many questions about the historic houses they were going to see.

Who cares about a bunch of old houses? Calvin thought. He hoped Dad was totally bored.

To prove how totally bored he was with old houses, Calvin peered over Jenny's shoulder. Of course, Jenny and Lola were turning the pages of a big book on magicians. Of course, the top of Jenny's paper read CLASS PROJECT.

"Now that I'm a money-making, *professional* magician," Jenny explained to Lola, "I need a good stage name."

Calvin read the names of famous magicians in Jenny's book. The Great Houdini, the Great Blackstone, the Great Thurston.

"Hey, Jenny!" Calvin grinned. "You can be the

Great"—his grin got wider—"the Great . . . Teiteltot!"

"I'll think about a stage name later." Jenny spoke to Lola and carefully ignored Calvin. "Right now I have to work on my *class project.*"

"The Great Teiteltot." Calvin savored the name. "It sounds like a little snack."

Jenny turned to her paper. She underlined "class project" three times.

Calvin squirmed. He didn't want to think about his class project. He shut up about the Great Teiteltot.

Jenny wrote down the names of six magicians.

Calvin squirmed even more. *Six* magicians. Why did Jenny always work so hard?

"Why not do your report on *one* magician?" Calvin suggested. "Why write about the whole magic squad?"

"Because I want to do extra—" Jenny stopped writing. "What did you say?"

Calvin took a deep breath. Jenny was actually interested in his advice! "I said, 'Why not—' "

"No, the last part."

Calvin racked his brain. "You mean, 'magic squad'?"

"Magic squad." Jenny almost smiled. "That's a great stage name."

Calvin thought about the name. There was one problem with it. " 'Squad' means a group," he pointed out. "Or at least more than one. In your act, there's only you."

"Maybe there *is* more than one," Jenny said.

Calvin shook his head. "Not unless you count Blackstone."

"Well, I am counting Blackstone," said Jenny. "And maybe one other person. I need an assistant."

Calvin barely heard Jenny because he was watching Train. The big dog circled his water dish three times and flopped to the ground. Train seemed no closer to learning how to come, sit, and heel than when he arrived. Going for a walk with him was still like chasing the Train.

Calvin let Coltrane's "Chasin' the Trane" song roll through his mind.

"Calvin!" Jenny said. "Don't you want to know who my assistant will be?"

She paused.

He didn't answer.

"It's you!" Jenny exclaimed, as if awarding Calvin a prize. "My new assistant is *you!*"

The last Coltrane notes faded from Calvin's brain. "*What?*"

"Who," Jenny corrected. " 'Who' is you."

" 'Who' is *not* me," Calvin said firmly. "Find someone else."

Jenny sighed. "There is no one else. Monk can't remember one card from the next, and Lola is too . . ." Jenny glanced at the small girl and carefully spelled, "L-I-T-T-L-E."

"I am *not* little," said Lola indignantly. "I'm almost five."

"That's right," Jenny soothed, then took a deep breath. "Calvin, I'll pay you ten dollars."

"Double it," said Calvin.

"Twenty dol—" Jenny struggled. "You're just the assistant!"

"*Just* the assistant." Calvin shook his head. "Oh well."

"Twenty dollars!" Jenny took another deep breath. "Okay, okay, but you have to practice with me every day."

Calvin agreed that was fair. Jenny then explained that an assistant handed props—scarves, wands, cards—to the magician during the magic act. "And," she finished, "the assistant has to wear a costume."

Calvin looked at the photos in Jenny's book. There were many men in tuxedos and top hats. There were many women, too. They wore big smiles and tiny, shiny clothes.

"Okay," said Calvin. "I'll wear a tuxedo and top hat."

"The tux and top hat are worn by the magician," said Jenny, "who in this case happens to be *me*. You have to wear . . . the assistant's clothes."

Calvin glanced at the array of tiny, shiny outfits. He pictured himself in a sequin-studded swimsuit.

"No," he said, shuddering.

Jenny looked from Calvin to the shiny clothes. She didn't even argue. "I wouldn't wear those things, either," she said.

"How about my red T-shirt?" Calvin suggested.

"Not that old wrinkled thing," cried Jenny. "Buy a new one. I want the Magic Squad to look very . . . professional."

Calvin beamed. He had a vision of himself,

professional in a new T-shirt, handing props to Jenny.

"And remember," Jenny cautioned, interrupting his vision, "you have to practice every day. You can't put it off till the last minute."

Calvin nodded before he realized he had been insulted. "Wait a minute," he said. "What do I put off till the last minute?"

"Most things," said Jenny. "Your project, for example."

Just as Calvin was about to explain that his project was being *carefully* planned, thank you very much, Dad drove up with Monk.

"What did you do this afternoon, sport?" Dad asked as Jenny and Calvin climbed into the backseat.

Calvin thought about the afternoon. "Well," he said, waving good-bye to Alfred Ludlott, who was at the window. "Jenny and I were just talking about our projects."

"That's great!" Dad exclaimed. "Sounds like you're really planning ahead. Tell me more."

"Well"—Calvin thought quickly—"I'm going to do posters on different dog breeds. And a list of how kids can help homeless animals."

"And what else?" asked Jenny.

"*And* . . . and . . . a bunch of other stuff," Calvin finished lamely.

"Do you need any help?" Dad asked.

"No, no," Calvin said quickly. "I want it to be a surprise."

Dad smiled. "I'll look forward to seeing the finished product."

"So will I," murmured Jenny.

"Monk and I had an interesting trip." Dad was so excited he forgot to start the car. "This city has some wonderful old houses! Did you know that the Curtis mansion is made of four different kinds of stone?"

"No," said Calvin.

"Dad, I think"—Monk looked up from his book and smiled his faraway smile—"I think it was actually *five* kinds of stone."

"Five, that's right," said Dad. "Calvin, would you like to see the Curtis mansion? Maybe this weekend? I know Mom would love to go. Monk can point out the stones."

"No," Calvin said quietly. He didn't want Monk to point out the stones. He didn't want to go on a secondhand TAG trip.

"Well, maybe another time. You know," Dad said, patting Monk's shoulder, "there's a lot I never learned, but thanks to you three smart, hardworking kids, maybe I'll start to catch up."

Calvin stared out the car window, not even seeing the wag-wag-wag of Train's skinny tail. He knew Monk was smart. Jenny was hardworking. But he wasn't sure where he fit in.

"Roo-roo-roo," Train called a good-bye.

Calvin saw Alfred Ludlott slam down the window.

6

On Monday Calvin read his dog-training books all over again. Why was Train so difficult to train? He still did not come. He did not sit or heel. He had not yet learned the meaning of "quiet."

Another week passed.

Train *still* did not come. He did not sit or heel. His bark was as loud as ever.

Maybe he's mixed up, Calvin thought, because he's a mixed-breed dog. Maybe the terrier genes are confusing the hound genes, which are confusing the pointer and German shepherd genes.

Calvin continued to work hard, though, and look worried. Train worked hard, too, and looked confused. Each time Calvin called a command— "Come!" "Sit!" "Heel!"—Train's ears pricked, his pink tongue lolled, and he rushed . . . to do the wrong thing. Calvin just sighed and started again.

In addition to training Train, Calvin was being trained by Jenny. Sometimes he thought "train" was the only word in his vocabulary. His grass-lying, Coltrane-listening days were over. As Monk read or talked with Alfred Ludlott, Calvin learned to hand Jenny the right props—wand, scarf, plastic flower—at exactly the right moment. Lola watched and loudly corrected his mistakes.

Blackstone, Jenny's white guinea pig, was to be an important part of the birthday magic show. Blackstone had regular evening training sessions at Jenny's apartment because Jenny could not bring the guinea pig to Alfred Ludlott's house after school. Calvin would not actually work with Blackstone until the day of the show.

Until then, Jenny used a Blackstone substitute.

A fuzzy bedroom slipper.

Which seemed appropriate, Calvin thought, because Blackstone did indeed resemble a slipper.

"Calvin, *don't* grab like that," Jenny scolded. "You're squeezing Blackstone's head."

Calvin decided to have some fun. He juggled the slipper like a hot potato.

"That's *Blackstone*," Jenny and Lola shrieked.

Calvin tossed the slipper high. It did a few flips, swan dives, and loop-de-loops. It swooped like a fuzzy acrobat.

"Watch this! Watch this!" Calvin balanced the slipper on his nose, like a seal. "A*arr, aarr*," he barked, clapping his hands.

Plop! The slipper flopped, tip first, to the grass.

"Whoops," said Calvin.

Jenny snatched up the slipper and made a great show of dusting and smoothing and cooing to it.

"You're *fired*," screamed Lola.

"You have one last chance." Jenny glared, gently scratching the slipper. "You must treat Blackstone with respect."

"That old slip—"

"It's the *pretend* Blackstone," said Jenny. Then she added significantly, "Remember, *twenty* dollars."

Calvin just sighed. He reached for the slipper—the *pretend* Blackstone—and carefully cradled it.

Another Monday, the beginning of yet another week. They're coming too quickly, Calvin thought, as he snapped a leash to Train's collar. What if he

couldn't train Train in time? What if Train had to return to the shelter? Calvin squished down these thoughts. Train was smart. He had great potential. Surely he would be trained in a few more days.

In Alfred Ludlott's yard, Train pranced at the end of his leash. He pranced around Calvin.

"Heel," Calvin called, whirling around. "Come! Good boy! Sit!"

Train pranced faster, round and round.

"Heel!" cried Calvin, spinning too.

"Roo-roo," called Train, increasing his pace. He seemed to think Calvin was playing a game.

Calvin spun faster and faster. The grass, the leaves, the trees spun, too. Faster, faster, faster.

Plunk! Calvin sat down hard.

The grass whirled up, the sky spun down. Train seemed to leap in twenty places at once. Calvin shook his head to clear the dizziness.

He could see Monk sitting cross-legged in his usual nose-in-a-book position.

He saw one girl-sized pair of red sneakers and a tiny, skipping pair. He watched the first pair start to move—backward.

Huh? thought Calvin. He shook his head harder to clear out the last dizzy spin.

"Roo-roo," called Train.

Calvin scrutinized those sneakers. He watched their backward motion. Finally he looked up.

"*Aargh!*" he cried.

The sneakers were Jenny's, the tuxedo was Jenny's, the hair was Jenny's, the face . . . The face was the oddest Calvin had ever seen.

There were green triangles around the eyes, red dots on the cheeks, and a red mouth thick with lipstick.

"Hey, Jenny!" Calvin hollered, jumping to his feet. "Trick or treat!"

Jenny ignored him. She began pushing at the air. It looked like she was patting a box.

Except there was no box to be seen.

Monk stared, openmouthed. He lifted a finger to his right ear and twirled it around and around. "Cuckoo," he pronounced.

Calvin nodded. Jenny's constant magic had finally driven her cuckoo.

With Train straining at the leash, Calvin pressed forward. He waved both hands in front of Jenny's blank face.

"Jenny," he called. "Jenny!"

Silence. Jenny continued to pat the absent box.

Train tried to help. He pawed Jenny's tuxedo legs.

"*Calvin,*" said Jenny, crossly and very clearly. "Call off that dog."

"What a relief," said Calvin as Train drooled on Jenny's shoes. "You're okay."

"Of course I'm okay." Jenny dusted off paw prints. "I was being a mime."

"A *mind?*" Calvin asked, sure that Jenny had lost hers. He had seen pictures of minds—well, brains, to be exact. They were gray and wrinkled, like old fruit. Jenny did not look one bit like a mind.

"A *mime*. M-I-M-E." Jenny rolled her triangle eyes. "A mime is an artistic clown."

"Oh, you'd be a good clown." Calvin grinned.

"A mime doesn't talk," Jenny continued.

"Doesn't talk," teased Calvin. "Oh, you'd be no good at that."

Jenny explained mimes to Calvin, Monk, and Lola, whose gaze never wavered from those triangle eyes. Jenny told them that the mime face was like a mask, and that ancient Greek actors were the first mimes. The art had been refined in Italy, and some of the world's best mimes were French.

"Mimes are like dancers," said Jenny, "because

they can create a whole world through their movements, without using words!"

"A world without words!" Monk bristled. "What's wrong with words?"

Calvin repeated the last part of Jenny's sentence: "They create a whole world . . . without using words." He didn't know any kid—Jenny included—who talked like that.

Calvin cocked a skeptical eyebrow. "Jenny," he said, "did you get all that from a book?"

"For your information," Jenny said with great dignity, "I met a mime—a real mime—at Buster's Magic Shop on Saturday."

The mime had helped Jenny pick out mime makeup and a book on mime routines. "The mime showed me how to make green triangle eyes," said Jenny. "The mime showed me how to walk backward. The mime suggested that I combine magic with mime to create a truly unique performance. That's what the mime said—'truly unique performance.' See my makeup? It's different from most mimes' whiteface because I'm a mime-*magician.*"

Mime this, mime that, thought Calvin. Mime, mime, mime. For a silent mime, Jenny sure had a lot to say.

Suddenly Calvin had an idea.

He had agreed to be an assistant to a *magician*. Being an assistant to a mime-magician would be more difficult. Why, it was like having two jobs!

Calvin told Jenny he wanted a raise.

This time it was Jenny who cocked the skeptical eyebrow. "Let me get this straight," she said. "You want more money just because I'm silent."

"Yes." Calvin nodded eagerly.

"Hmmm." Jenny studied the dog drool on her right sneaker. "I'm not sure a *mime*-magician really needs an assistant."

"Er," said Calvin.

"In fact"—Jenny studied the dog drool on the left sneaker—"an assistant might be totally unnecessary."

"But—but—" cried Calvin. In his mind, he saw all his hard assistant work vanishing—*poof*! "Your stage name is Magic Squad," he reminded Jenny. "And *squad* means a group, or at least more than one."

Jenny scanned first one dog-drooly sneaker, then the other. "Hmmm," she said again.

Calvin waited anxiously.

"Oh well." Jenny shrugged. "I'll probably need

your help for this show anyway, since we've already practiced. You can still be my assistant."

"About that raise—?"

"No," said Jenny.

Calvin decided not to push it.

CALVIN DID NOT USUALLY THINK AHEAD UNLESS HE was counting the days till his birthday or Christmas. Each week he counted the days till Friday. Each school day he counted the hours till lunch. But he rarely thought about the future, much less worried about it.

Now he was starting to think about the future, Train's future.

And he was starting to worry.

Train still was not very well trained. In fact, most days, Train seemed completely *un*trained.

Today was one of those days.

When Calvin snapped the leash to Train's collar, the big dog surged ahead, chuffing like a locomotive. Calvin trailed like a slow caboose.

Chasing the Train, Calvin thought.

"Chasin' the Trane." He let the big sound of Coltrane's song play through his mind as Train chugged him across the yard.

How could the week be passing so quickly? Calvin squished down the question. He did not want to think about time going by. That meant another week was almost over, and Train was no closer to—

"Roo-roo," Train called to a napping Fitzgerald.

"Quiet," said Calvin, tugging the leash.

"*Roo!*" Train tried again, but the dachshund barely opened one eye.

Even though he usually trained Train in Alfred Ludlott's yard, Calvin had decided that today they would travel around the neighborhood. Maybe Train needed a change to help him learn, Calvin thought. Maybe he needed an enriching trip.

Today Monk was on a TAG trip, *another* TAG trip. This time his class was going to see a perfor-mance of Shakespeare's play *Hamlet*. After the show, they would talk with the actors and examine the costumes, stage, and lights.

Of course, Dad had gotten very excited. At last night's dinner table, he had asked Monk lots of questions. Then he had mournfully addressed his fork. " 'Life's but . . . a poor player,' " he had droned to the pea skewered pitifully there.

"Actually, Dad"—Monk had given his slow, sweet smile—"those lines are from *Macbeth*, not *Hamlet*. Alfred Ludlott read them to me."

"To pea or not to pea," Mom intoned to the small green pile on her plate. "That is the question."

"Just one word off, Mom," Monk said, clapping. "But you've got the right play."

Mom bowed with a flourish and winked at Dad.

But being wrong only increased Dad's excitement. "There's so much I never learned." He banged his fork for emphasis. *Squish*, went the pea. "I goofed around in school," Dad continued. "You boys have great potential. Don't do less than you can. Right, Monk?"

"Sure," Monk agreed absently, reading the label on a loaf of bread.

"Right, Calvin?"

Calvin merely nodded. He felt as full of potential as that small, squished pea. A squished pea beside Monk's giant beanstalk of potential. A C kind of guy who couldn't even teach a dog to come.

Of course Dad had left work early to go with the TAG class to the performance. Sometimes Calvin thought Dad should be the TAG in the family, not Monk. Calvin could tell that most of the trips didn't really interest Monk. The boy would much rather read at Alfred Ludlott's house or talk with the poet.

Most of the trips didn't really interest Calvin, either. But it would be—well, kind of nice if Dad asked him lots of questions. It would be nice to sit beside Dad on the school bus. It would be nice to choose a seat beside Dad at the theater, and maybe roll a few fine words off his tongue.

" 'Life's but . . . a poor player,' " Calvin murmured.

Train panted softly.

Calvin listened to the rhythmic click of Train's toenails on the sidewalk. Purple pansies dipped in a few yards, and a truck rumbled in the distance. Nothing marred the peaceful afternoon.

Then Calvin saw *it*. He tensed.

Train continued his tongue-lolling, lollygagging walk.

Then he saw *it*, too.

A little dog prancing down the street.

Train loved being friendly to other dogs.

"*Roo!*" He flung out a robust hello.

"Quiet," Calvin soothed. "Good dog. Good dog."

"Roo-roo." Train leaped against his leash. "Roo-roo-roo-roo."

The little dog kept coming. She did not even glance at Train. She looked as if she had a thousand better things to do than trade barks with a loud-rooing dog.

"Roo-roo-roo-roo!"

Train lunged. Calvin set his heels hard against the sidewalk. But, inch by inch, Train dragged him forward.

Calvin felt like a guy slow-surfing the concrete.

"Hello, Calvin," said a familiar voice.

Calvin looked up, panting. "Oh," he said. "Hello, Dr. Jamar."

"Do you remember Biscuit?"

"Biscuit!" Calvin looked down at the polite little dog. He knew why he hadn't recognized her at first.

Biscuit was no longer doing that pancake-dog act. She sat straight, without cowering. Wag-wag-wag went her stub of a tail.

"Biscuit has a new home," said Dr. Jamar. "In fact, I'm walking Biscuit to her new family right now." Dr. Jamar waved a big shopping bag filled with dog bowls, toys, and treats. "I'm taking her things, too," Dr. Jamar explained. "A few familiar toys and treats will help her feel at home."

Wag-wag-wag, went Biscuit's tail.

"Roo-roo-roo," went Train.

"*Quiet!*" hollered a woman from an open window.

"Train," pleaded Calvin, tugging the leash. "Train, please, please, *please* be quiet."

Suddenly Dr. Jamar whispered, "Calvin, Calvin, Calvin." She gently pulled his sleeve.

Huh? thought Calvin.

"Calvin, Calvin, Calvin," Dr. Jamar whispered again. She jerked his sleeve in a different direction.

"*What?*" said Calvin.

"Calvin," Dr. Jamar said once, firmly. She tugged his sleeve once.

"Calvin," she repeated in the same brisk voice. She tugged his sleeve again, in the same direction.

Calvin grinned. "Roo-roo-roo," he said.

Dr. Jamar grinned, too, then said, "Being consistent and clear is very important in training. You don't want to confuse your dog." Dr. Jamar took the leash from Calvin and handed him Biscuit's leash.

"Come," she called firmly to Train. "Train, come."

The big dog pranced to her side and flattened his ears for a pat, then wandered again to the end of his leash.

"Train," Dr. Jamar called. She tugged the leash once. "Train, come."

Train came immediately.

Calvin felt a glow of hope. "Dr. Jamar," he said, "now that Biscuit has a new home maybe *you* can foster Train."

"There's no need for that," Dr. Jamar said. "I can tell you've treated him kindly, and you're off to a good start with his training. Just remember to be clear, firm, and consistent."

"I've *tried*," Calvin said, "but he doesn't come for me. He doesn't do *anything* for me, and there's not enough time—"

"Calvin." Dr. Jamar fixed him with one eye. "This dog has great potential."

"Yes," Calvin agreed miserably.

"And so"—Dr. Jamar winked—"do you."

69

CALVIN WAS TIRED OF HEARING ABOUT HIS GREAT potential. He kept hearing about it from Dad. And now Dr. Jamar was telling him the same thing. Besides, he was too busy with Train's potential to think about his own. Calvin sighed as Train tugged him back to Alfred Ludlott's yard.

Calvin poured fresh water into Train's bowl and watched as the big dog drank. Then he wandered over to an impatient Jenny for his umpteenth training session. He felt he could hand her that bedroom slipper in his sleep, but Jenny still was not satisfied. "I want the Magic Squad to be *perfect*," she said.

As Calvin practiced the magic act, he tried not to think about Train's poor training. Calvin's thoughts jumped around. He thought of Dad's happy talk about Monk's TAG work and Calvin's project. He thought of Dad buying dog magazines, poster paper, scissors. "Calvin, I'm proud of you," Dad kept saying. "I've never seen you work so hard. I can't wait to see your final project. The school year is off to a good start. You have great potential." Talk, talk, talk. Dad's proud words fell around Calvin like snow. Sometimes he felt smothered under the weight of so much talk, talk, talk on potential.

He did not feel like he had great potential. He felt like a fake.

"Jenny," he asked suddenly, "how much work have you done on your project?"

With eyes closed, Jenny waved her wand and—whoosh!—a red scarf appeared.

"What?" she asked.

"Your project," said Calvin. "Are you almost finished?"

"Oh, yeah," said Jenny, waving her wand again. "I'm totally finished, but I want to do an extra section on mimes. I'm typing it on my mother's computer."

Show-off, Calvin thought, but he didn't say the

71

word out loud. He knew it wasn't really true. Jenny liked to do big projects. Usually she got As on them.

Calvin didn't care about Jenny's grades. Usually he didn't care that much about his own grades.

But somehow this project wasn't about grades. Calvin wished Dad would quit asking questions, would quit making comments, would quit smiling proudly as if he had another TAG son.

"I am *not* Monk," Calvin murmured, clenching his fist.

"*Calvin!*" Jenny shrieked. "You're *killing* Blackstone."

Calvin looked down. In his fierce grip flopped the limp, fuzzy slipper.

"Sorry," he said, smoothing the pretend Blackstone.

"You're not paying attention," Jenny scolded.

"I'm *thinking*."

"Just keep thinking twenty dollars," grumbled Jenny. "Lola's party is two days away."

"I know." Calvin returned the slipper to Jenny. "Sorry about practice today. I've got a lot on my mind."

Jenny hesitated. "Calvin," she said gently, "our

projects are due the Monday after Lola's party. I mean, when are you . . . ?"

"Plenty of time," Calvin said heartily, pushing the Monday date out of his mind. Right now, training Train was his big project. Once that was finished, he'd have time to whip off a *dozen* school projects.

The next day Calvin decided to work with Train in the yard. He carefully followed Dr. Jamar's advice. He kept his commands clear and consistent.

"Come, Train," Calvin called briskly.

And Train came.

On the twelfth straight time that Train obeyed, Calvin heard clapping.

"Well done, Calvin!" Alfred Ludlott continued to applaud. "Train is finally learning."

"You should clap for Train," said Calvin. "He's the one doing the work."

The poet directed his clapping at Train, whose pink tongue happily lolled.

"Maybe," Calvin suggested hopefully, "maybe you'd like to keep him."

Alfred Ludlott stopped clapping. "Calvin," he said, "we've already had this discussion—"

"I know," said Calvin, "but I was hoping . . ."

The poet shook his head. "I already have one dog."

"Train would be company for Fitzgerald."

"His bark—"

"Has gotten quieter!"

"No." Alfred Ludlott shook his head very firmly. "His bark has *not* gotten quieter. Train is very distracting when I try to write."

"Oh," said Calvin. In a small voice, he asked, "*Very* distracting?"

"Yes," said Alfred Ludlott. "*Very* distracting. For one month I agreed to foster that dog—"

"Train," said Calvin. "His name is Train."

"For one month," Alfred Ludlott repeated, "I agreed to foster Train, and during that time you were supposed to find him a *permanent* home. I've kept my side of the agreement, but, Calvin, you have to keep yours."

Calvin nodded solemnly. He knew that if he didn't find a permanent home for Train (and soon), the dog would have to return to the humane shelter.

Calvin pictured the shelter. In his mind, he saw

the big and small dogs waiting for homes. He heard their excited barks.

Maybe now that he was (almost) trained, Train would have a better chance of finding a good home if he returned to the shelter.

But Train was no cute, plump puppy. Most people wanted puppies, and Train was a full-grown dog. He took up a lot of room. He ate a lot of food. He had, Calvin sadly acknowledged, a loud, a *very* loud, bark.

9

CALVIN HEARD TRAIN'S LOUD BARK ON SATURDAY, the day of Lola's party. He heard that loud bark again and again and again.

"Roo-roo," Train greeted each arriving car.

"Roo-roo," he announced each guest.

Calvin had decided to advertise Train at Lola's party. Everyone knew that little kids just *loved* dogs. And what parent could resist a dog as lovable as Train?

As he opened the front door to each parent, guest, and birthday gift, Calvin would point to the cardboard sign he had taped by the knob. Large letters spelled out:

DOG FOR FREE.
FRIENDLY, L♥VES CHILDREN

Calvin had even made the "o" in "loves" a fat, red heart. He had never, ever used "o"-hearts in the past, but Train's fate was growing desperate. If a fat, red heart helped Train find a new home, then Calvin would happily print a hundred—no, a *thousand*—signs filled with those silly "o"-hearts.

"Wouldn't you like a dog, a very nice dog?" he asked each parent at the door.

And the harried mother or father would wince at the loud roo-roos coming from the backyard, take one deep breath, and say, "*That* dog? No thanks."

"He's an excellent watchdog," Calvin tried to persuade one man.

"His bark," said the man, "is very loud."

"All the better," replied Calvin. "You want to be able to *hear* him."

"What did you say?" The man covered his ears. "I can't hear you above the noise."

"Never mind," said Calvin.

"Roo-roo-roo," said Train.

Calvin handed the man's daughter a bag of party candy. He couldn't understand why no one wanted a lovable watchdog like Train. Grown-ups were always worried about crime. Train, with his heroic, very loud bark, wouldn't let a thief get within forty feet of a house.

"Happy birthday!" screamed the little girl. She beaned Calvin with a green M&M, hopped over his foot, and raced away.

"Good luck with that dog," the man murmured as he hurried off the front porch.

Sighing, Calvin handed a bag to the next birthday guest.

"Nigel," said the mother, "thank the nice young man for your candy."

"No," said Nigel, gripping the bag.

"Ni-*gel*." The mother's voice rose.

"No." Nigel stuck his tongue out at Calvin.

"That's okay," Calvin said quickly.

"You are *so* polite," said Nigel's mother, "unlike one other young man here."

Nigel crammed candy into his mouth.

Calvin decided not to point out his sign to this particular kid. There are *homes*, he thought, and there are *good* homes. He wanted Train to have a *good* home.

When Calvin turned to the next birthday guest, he felt an M&M bonk the back of his head.

It was going to be a l-o-n-g party.

Later, in the dining room, Alfred Ludlott and Monk drifted with dazed eyes through the birthday-party mess. Torn paper littered the floor; M&M's whizzed through the air.

"I'm getting too old for this," Alfred Ludlott murmured. *Pop!* A pink balloon burst by his chin.

Ha! thought Calvin, with satisfaction. After this, how could the poet think Train was loud?

"Magic show! Magic show!" Calvin hollered, herding the kids into the living room.

Lola sat proudly in the place of honor in front of the magic table. With her black tights, black shirt, and red sneakers, she looked like a miniature Jenny.

And she could be as tough as Jenny. "*Sit* down and *shut* up," she ordered the noisy kids, and they immediately sat and hushed.

Jenny stood at her table beside a Magic Squad sign. With her top hat, red lips, and green triangle eyes, she looked very professional, Calvin thought. She looked, he imagined, like a true mime-magician.

Calvin ran his hands down his jeans, black to match Jenny's tuxedo. He fingered the collar of his new red T-shirt. He, Calvin Hastings, was part of this act. He was a member of the Magic Squad.

Suddenly Calvin felt nervous. What if he messed up? He took a few deep breaths and joined Jenny behind the table.

The little kids gazed up expectantly.

"Hey!" Nigel addressed Jenny. "You look weird."

Jenny ignored him.

"Weirdo! Weirdo!" Nigel hollered.

Jenny tightened her lips.

"She's a mime," Calvin explained.

"A *mind*?" Nigel asked.

"A *mime*," Calvin repeated. "M-I-M-E. A mime doesn't speak."

"Doesn't speak?" Nigel asked. "What if I kicked her?"

"She still wouldn't speak," said Calvin, "but don't even think about trying."

Lola glared at Nigel. "Quiet!" she said.

"I'm a guest," Nigel pouted. "I can talk if I want."

"No, you can't."

"Yes, I can."

"No—"

"Now, now, children," came Alfred Ludlott's frantic voice. "Let's not fight."

"She started—"

80

But at that moment, Jenny began the Magic Squad act.

First she gently waved her hands; then, looking surprised, she plucked an imaginary flower from the air. She stroked its imaginary petals, fingered its imaginary leaves. When she sniffed its imaginary scent . . . why, Calvin could practically *see* that flower. Right on time, he passed Jenny a scarf and held his breath.

The scarf flowed across Jenny's hand.

Whoosh! A perfect daisy appeared.

With a bow, Jenny presented the real flower to the birthday girl. Lola nodded her thanks and clutched it with both small hands.

"That's dumb," snorted Nigel.

Jenny moved smoothly to her next trick, pretending she was inside a big box.

As she patted the sides of the big, imaginary box, Calvin peered into the small, real box on Jenny's table. Inside, Blackstone, the guinea pig, scuttled. Her delicate whiskers shook.

"Shhh, shhh," Calvin whispered.

Then came the moment when Calvin was to give Jenny the real box containing the guinea pig. To do this, he had to stand on the table and hand the real box down to Jenny in the imaginary box. He had to be careful not to break through the imaginary sides.

Calvin lifted Blackstone's box. He could hear quick guinea pig movements inside. He carefully climbed on top of the table.

Spellbound, the children watched the real box. They, too, heard the quick movements. What surprise waited inside?

Openmouthed, miming surprise, Jenny reached up to accept the real box.

She tapped the imaginary box. No sound.

She tapped the real box. *Tap-tap-tap.*

Everyone waited.

Suddenly *thump-thump-thump* came from *inside* the box.

All the children leaned forward.

Calvin leaned forward, too. The fuzzy slipper had never been *this* exciting.

Jenny reached into the real box . . . and held up the white guinea pig.

With bright, beadlike eyes, Blackstone peered at the audience.

"Yay!" screamed the children. They leaped to their feet and started pushing forward.

Jenny shook her head and touched the sides of the imaginary box.

"The mime is still inside the box," Calvin warned. "You can go no closer."

Still balanced on top of the table, he handed a magic scarf down to Jenny.

The room grew completely still.

Jenny moved the scarf gently over the guinea pig. Once . . . twice. Each time, Blackstone emerged, nose working, from the folds of the scarf.

Jenny made a third pass, lifted the scarf . . .

And Blackstone had disappeared.

Perched on the table, Calvin wanted to cheer. The most difficult trick had worked! It had worked *perfectly*.

Several children started to wail.

"I want to pat it," cried a little girl.

"Bring it back," commanded another.

"We'll find that . . . creature!" Nigel waved a plastic spoon like a sword. "Forward to victory, men!"

And like a general leading his troops into battle, Nigel advanced on the box.

"Get back! Get back!" Calvin shouted as kids stormed through the imaginary sides.

"Get back! Get back!" Jenny yelled, flapping her magic scarf.

"That mime," one girl said, "is talking."

"That mime," Nigel said, "is a fake."

Jenny's imaginary box could not withstand the onslaught.

"Calvin!" Jenny shrieked, gripping her scarf. "Calvin, *save* Blackstone!"

Calvin reached down to her uplifted hands.

Two dozen birthday-guest bodies rammed at his table.

Calvin grabbed for the guinea pig.

His table slipped.

"I see it! I see it!" shrilled someone.

Calvin's feet did a desperate tap dance

down,

down,

down—

"Yow!" he yelled. His hands reached for the frightened Blackstone.

And closed on empty air.

The table crashed to the ground.

But the kids were off and running.

"I see it! I see it!" Nigel shouted. "Forward! Forward, men!"

"Yay!" screamed the children.

From the floor, Calvin caught a glimpse of Blackstone's furry rump, then dozens of small, swift shoes.

"Be still! Stay quiet!" Jenny cried, racing after them.

"Children, children!" Alfred Ludlott called, caught in a swirl of ribbon.

Calvin became aware of two little red sneakers right in his line of vision. He looked up past black tights, black shirt hem. . . . He saw two small hands firmly planted on small hips.

Lola Ludlott glared down at him.

"My birthday," she snapped, coldly clipping each word. "My *fifth* birthday . . . is *ruined*. Totally, totally *ruined*."

And with that, she stomped off to help save Blackstone.

Carefully, Calvin got to his feet and rubbed a bruised shin. Ouch! From this angle, he could see part of the back door. He heard Train give a half-hearted "roo."

Then he heard the drumroll sound of racing feet. The kids were fast approaching. The sound got louder, louder. They were headed for the door.

"We'll get that varmint yet!" Calvin heard Nigel's voice. Apparently the kid had switched from tough general to tough cowboy. Calvin grimaced and shook his head.

And then he saw Blackstone.

The guinea pig was huddled in a corner by the door, half hidden by birthday paper.

"Shhh, shhh." Calvin moved slowly toward the little animal.

Rustle, rustle: Blackstone cowered against the paper.

"Don't worry, Blackstone," Calvin soothed. "I won't hurt you."

"Okay, men!" Nigel's voice came again. "We're getting close to that sneaky critter. Let's post scouts in every room. Megan, you take the stairs; Bruce, the bathroom. I'll search—"

Calvin saw a grubby hand reach for the back-door knob.

"Don't open—" he yelled.

But Nigel had twisted the knob and pulled.

"—the door," Calvin whispered.

Blackstone shot through the open space— safety!—and tumbled down the stairs. Nigel rushed after, then Calvin.

In the yard, Train watched the commotion with interest. He had been feeling lonely. Earlier this afternoon, not one of those fascinating small and large strangers had stopped to give him a pat.

Now perhaps they were coming to play.

Train liked to play. His whines changed to excited barks. He saw Calvin and wagged his tail.

Then he glimpsed something else.

Was it a ball, this white, fuzzy thing zooming toward him? What could it possibly be?

Train's lopsided ears went up.

He caught a whiff of rabbitlike scent.

And the hunter in him came out.

"Roo-roo." He bared his teeth. "Roo-roo-roo-roo."

Calvin could only watch, horrified.

His mind went blank. He could not think of a single command.

He heard Jenny yell, the little kids scream.

Blind with fear, the guinea pig raced straight for the barking Train.

Calvin saw the big dog lunge.

Train hurtled toward the oncoming guinea pig.

His black nose worked the air.

He was so intent, he didn't even bark. He was a flash of powerful muscle.

Then Calvin saw Train do something he had never seen before.

The big dog stretched his whole body, from his nose to his tail, and lifted his right front paw.

Train froze into a perfect point.

He pointed straight at his doghouse. And there, from the door of that doghouse, peered . . . a trembling Blackstone.

"Good dog! *Good* dog!" Calvin grabbed Train's collar and stroked his big head. "Your pointer genes came out!"

Jenny snatched Blackstone from the depths of the doghouse. The guinea pig cuddled against her as Jenny stroked the quivering fur. "Blackstone's heart is beating about a thousand times a minute," Jenny murmured to Calvin as she soothed the frightened animal. "No more little-kid parties for Blackstone. They are way too stressful."

Nigel planted himself squarely in front of Calvin and Train. "Hey, I want to pat this dog."

He reached out and thumped Train's back.

"Don't do that," Calvin said angrily when Train jumped. "Be gentle."

"Is he your dog?"

"Well . . . not really."

"Then I'm going to pat him." Nigel thumped at Train again, then peered into Train's brown eyes.

"Look! He likes me!" Train's tail gave a half-hearted wag. "I'm going to tell my mother to buy me this dog."

"He's not—" Calvin hotly began.

"—for sale." Alfred Ludlott appeared suddenly beside Calvin. "He's for free."

"For free!" Nigel shouted, climbing on Train's broad back.

Parents began arriving to pick up their children.

The l-o-n-g party was almost over. Nigel's mother picked her way across the grass. "Nigel dear," she murmured, "that sweet doggy is not a horse."

"Yes, he is," shouted Nigel. "Giddyup." He clapped a palm to the confused dog's side.

"Be gentle," murmured Nigel's mother as Calvin removed the kicking kid. She turned to Alfred Ludlott. "Nigel and your dog seem to be good friends already. I've been thinking about getting him a pet. Nigel *dotes* on animals."

"I can see that," Calvin muttered, loosening Nigel's grip on the poor dog's ears. "Ow!" he yelped as Nigel delivered a kick to his leg.

Nigel's mother continued to murmur and smile. "Such a sweet, sweet dog. Are you *sure* you want to give him away?"

"Oh, *yes.*" Alfred Ludlott nodded. "*Yes.* Indeed, *yes.*"

Calvin did not like the way the poet emphasized the word "yes." Anyone would think the man did not like Train. Just because the dog had barked a few times and dug a little hole . . .

"Train is a big dog," Calvin said loudly. "He needs a big yard."

Nigel surveyed Alfred Ludlott's lawn. "My yard is bigger," he proclaimed. "Much bigger."

"Marvelous." Alfred Ludlott beamed.

"What a sweet sight." Nigel's mother smiled at her son, who again was fiercely riding the dog.

Calvin snorted. "Having a dog is not all play," he said. "Train must be walked and fed every day. *Every . . . single . . . day.*" There, he thought. The poet wasn't the only one who could emphasize words.

The mother's smile widened when she heard those emphasized words. "Oh!" she exclaimed. "I've been trying to teach Nigel responsibility. A dog might be *just* what he needs."

"Train is a *big* responsibility," Calvin emphasized.

"I *love* him!" Nigel tightly hugged the dog.

"His *bark,*" Calvin emphasized grimly, "is *very* loud."

"But you get used to it," responded Alfred Ludlott.

"A watchdog!" Nigel's mother actually clapped her hands. "Why, this dog is *perfect.*"

"I don't think you'll be disappointed," said Alfred Ludlott. "Old Fitzgerald, here, is a wonderful companion. One of my dearest friends."

Fitzgerald huddled closer to Alfred Ludlott's leg. His face crinkled anxiously as he watched Nigel rough-loving Train.

"Oh, I'm sure you're right," Nigel's mother responded to the poet. "That big dog is *so* well behaved."

"Calvin deserves the credit for that." Alfred Ludlott draped an arm around Calvin's shoulder.

Calvin stiffened. He did not want Alfred Ludlott's praise.

The poet continued, "When he first came, Train was a big . . . nuisance. But Calvin saw his potential and patiently—very patiently—trained him. Why, now he'd be welcome in anyone's house."

"I'm going to name him Warrior," Nigel shouted.

"Or something nicer," murmured the mother. "How about Sweetie, or Pork Chop?"

"His name," Calvin said, "is Train."

"Name is a name is a name," soothed the poet, "to paraphrase the great Gertrude Stein. It doesn't make any difference—"

"It *does* make a difference," said Calvin. "If you call him by a different name, Train will get confused."

"I'm sure it doesn't—" murmured the mother.

"*Any*one would get confused!" Calvin rounded on Alfred Ludlott. "What if people suddenly started calling you—" He glanced around wildly. "What if they suddenly started calling you *Dog Dish*? Wouldn't *you* get confused?"

"Calvin," said Alfred Ludlott, "I am not a dog."

"Neither am I," said Calvin. "But I'm trying to understand how a dog might feel. The least you can do is *try*." He remembered Biscuit, the little dog that Dr. Jamar had fostered. He remembered Biscuit's confusion and fear. Her owner—the friend she had lived with for years—had disappeared, had died. Calvin remembered how Biscuit would go flat, like a pancake, even when Dr. Jamar spoke kindly. Calvin understood *exactly* how Biscuit felt. He thought of all the changes waiting for Train: a new home, a strange owner. He hoped Train wouldn't be frightened. He hoped Train wouldn't want to go flat.

The least they can do, Calvin thought, is to let Train keep his name.

"Oh, who cares." Nigel's mother broke the silence. "If you want, we'll keep calling him Train."

"Warrior Train," said Nigel.

Calvin sighed. He had won, but he still felt he had lost.

Alfred Ludlott patted Calvin's shoulder. "We're glad you're offering Train a good home," the poet said to Nigel's mother. "Otherwise, he'd have to go back to the humane shelter."

No, he wouldn't, Calvin thought. He could stay here with you.

But all Calvin said aloud was, "I'll get Train's bowls and leash."

Calvin took a long time packing Train's things into a shopping bag, but finally he could no longer put off their good-bye. As he rubbed the dog's lopsided ears, Calvin explained that Nigel would be taking him to a new home.

"I thought Alfred Ludlott had great dog-owner potential," Calvin murmured. "I'm sorry it didn't work out."

He watched as Train was bundled into the strange car.

Beside Alfred Ludlott, Fitzgerald uttered a sharp little bark.

"Fitzgerald," Alfred Ludlott scolded, "are you picking up Train's bad habits?"

But Fitzgerald didn't bark again. He and Calvin watched silently till Train and the car were out of sight.

Calvin quietly helped the birthday guests find jackets and party favors. He discovered one bright yellow sock on top of a lamp and a hair bow inside the sink.

Jenny and Monk were quiet, too, as they threw away paper and ribbon. Blackstone, tired from her traumatic afternoon, dozed inside a box. Alfred Ludlott made a few cheery comments, then stopped. And Fitzgerald—well, Calvin could see his long dachshund face peering sadly from Train's doghouse.

When Dad picked them up, the three kids piled quietly into the car. Dad asked questions, tried a joke. Finally he asked, "What's wrong?"

"Train has a new home," said Calvin, staring out the window.

"But that's good," said Dad. "I thought that's what you wanted."

Jenny and Monk looked at Calvin, then looked at each other.

"Mr. Hastings," Jenny said, "Train's new owner is not a very nice kid."

"He kicks." Monk rolled down his sock, showing an angry red mark on his ankle.

"He kicks hard," said Dad. "That mark will turn into a bruise. I'll put ice on it when we get home, to ease the swelling."

Dad then turned to his oldest son. "That's too bad about Train," he said, "and after you spent so much time training him. How are you feeling?"

How did he feel? Calvin didn't know what to say. He remembered the words from some old poem Alfred Ludlott had read to Monk: "racked by despair."

Racked by despair.

Calvin wasn't sure what "racked" meant, but it sounded terrible. And "despair" must be this feeling: hollow and sad.

He had wanted to help Train find a good home, but instead the dog was living with a kid who screamed and kicked. Calvin's own leg throbbed from a Nigel kick.

Calvin didn't know how to explain what he was feeling, so he kept quiet during the ride home. Houses, humans, trees, dogs flashed by his window, but he didn't even notice. He was wishing he did not have to return to Alfred Ludlott's house next week after school.

The empty doghouse would remind him of Train.

The hole in the backyard would remind him of Train.

Even Fitzgerald—that small, sausage-shaped dog—would remind him of big, barking Train.

In four days, Ms. Eva would return from her jazz dance tour. Then Calvin, Jenny, and Monk would again stay with Ms. Eva after school. There would be no more afternoons at Alfred Ludlott's house. Monk might visit the poet. Jenny might visit Lola. But Calvin did not want to visit, ever. He would be happy never to return.

The day after Lola's party was Sunday. Usually Calvin liked Sundays. He liked to read the comics, watch some football, play with his hamster, Pizzazz.

But this Sunday was different. Empty. Calvin spread out the comics and plunked down on the floor. He kept forgetting to turn the page.

Calvin could hear Mom and Monk talking in the kitchen, talking about some TAG thing.

If he were supersmart like Monk, Calvin thought, then Train wouldn't be living now with some mean, kicking kid. Monk would have found the dog a perfect—an A+—home. At best, Train's new home with Nigel might get a D.

Dad rattled his newspaper and cleared his throat. Finally he cheerfully asked, "All finished with your project, Calvin?"

That *project* again. Calvin supposed it was time to start doing his research and working on his posters. But he really didn't feel like it. Not today.

"How did it turn out?" Dad continued.

"Um."

"Do you want to show it to me?"

"No," said Calvin softly.

His father looked hurt. "Why?"

"Because."

"Because what?"

"Because it's *stupid*," Calvin whispered. "My dog idea is stupid. Monk would do something brilliant. Jenny would do something interesting—"

"But you worked so hard," Dad interrupted.

"I did *not* work hard," Calvin yelled. "What's the use? I'll never be smart like Monk." He jumped up, scattering papers.

"What's the matter?" called Mom from the kitchen. "Is everything okay?"

"Calvin," said Dad. "Wait."

But Calvin had already run down the hall. *Bang!* went the door of his room.

Breathing fast, Calvin reached into his hamster's cage. Even the touch of Pizzazz's fur was soothing. The way the hamster snuggled into his palm eased that tight-hearted feeling.

Calvin lay back on the bed and let Pizzazz run across his chest. He felt Pizzazz's quick feet on his bare arm and a whisker kiss on his cheek.

Rap-rap-rap, came a knock at the door. Calvin recognized that knock.

Dad's knock.

"Calvin, may I come in?"

"No," said Calvin.

"I'd like to talk—"

"I'm working on my project," said Calvin as Pizzazz raced down his arm. "I can't be disturbed."

"I'll be back later," said Dad. "Then we need to talk."

Talk, talk, talk, Calvin thought. He didn't want to talk. He didn't want to do anything but lie flat on his back while the noon light dimmed. He lay for a long, long time.

Rappity-rap: Mom's knock at the door.

"Calvin, I know losing Train is hard. Sometimes it helps to talk . . ."

Ha! thought Calvin. How can talking help Train?

"Mom," he replied, "I can't talk. Not now. I just want to be alone."

Calvin watched the shadows creep over the ceiling. He patted his hamster buddy.

"I wanted Train to have a *good* home," Calvin told Pizzazz. "He deserves the best." Calvin's throat filled with a crying feeling.

In Calvin's palm the hamster twitched his whiskers, almost as if he agreed.

Finally Calvin sat up, returned Pizzazz to his cage, and fed the hamster some seeds.

Then he looked at the pile of dog magazines on the floor.

Project time.

Calvin picked up one magazine, flipped through it, and found a handsome collie.

He cut it out.

Or, rather, he chopped it out. He didn't care about the ragged edges or—*slash!*—the rip in the picture's ear.

He found a picture of a pointer. Train had some pointer in him, Calvin remembered; then he pushed the thought aside. Chop, chop, chop—and the pointer joined the collie.

Tap-tap-tap: Monk's knock at the door.

Calvin ignored it.

"Calvin, I need to come in. This is my room, too."

Calvin did not look up from his chopping. His throat felt hard and tight, and his heart felt all chopped, like the pictures.

"Get me some tape first," Calvin commanded. "From the kitchen drawer."

"Say please," said Monk.

Right now, Calvin did not want to say anything,

not one word. But he *especially* did not want to say please.

He shut his lips.

Finally he heard Monk's footsteps lollygag down the hall, then lollygag back.

Monk handed Calvin a roll of thick, brown tape, the kind used for heavy packages.

Calvin didn't even care that it was the wrong kind of tape. He tore off a big chunk, then stuck the collie picture to his poster.

"Calvin." Monk shifted from one foot to the other. "Do you want clear tape?"

"No," said Calvin, sticking another picture. "This is good enough."

Monk watched the tear-and-stick of more brown tape. "Calvin," he said in a low voice, "that looks really ugly."

"It doesn't matter," said Calvin.

Monk straightened his glasses. "Do you, um, want me to help?" he asked shyly. "I can find some good pictures."

"It doesn't matter," Calvin repeated through his tight throat.

Monk hesitated. "That's sad about Train and

all, Calvin," he said softly. "You trained him really well. Alfred Ludlott says you're real good with animals. Kind and patient. He says you have a gift."

"It doesn't matter." Calvin dashed a hand across his eyes. "I'm not sure I helped Train all that much."

"Maybe you did," said Monk, watching his brother hack out a husky. Calvin's only reply was the *chop-chop-chop* of his scissors.

When Monk finally slipped away, Calvin continued to chop, tear, and stick. He printed—and misspelled—the names of the dog breeds. His ink pen blotted and smeared, but Calvin didn't care. He was no TAG. He just wanted to finish.

Calvin propped the poster on his desk and stood back to get the full effect.

Without a doubt, his project was ugly. *Really* ugly.

If prizes were given, Calvin thought, for the sloppiest, *least* helpful project, then his would surely win. Well, at least he was done.

That was when Dad walked in.

Calvin heard his father's breath catch, then release in a slow sigh. "Calvin," said Dad, "you can do better than that."

"I can't." Calvin crossed his arms. "This is the best I can do."

"It's not," said Dad.

"I did it," said Calvin, "and I say it's my best."

"Calvin"—Dad spoke slowly, carefully—"I know you're not Monk. Learning comes easy to him. I know you have to work harder, study harder. I don't expect you to be Monk." Dad sighed. "But I do expect you to try."

"To try to be Monk?" Calvin asked. "I thought so."

A sad look flicked through Dad's eyes. "To try to do your best," he said, sitting heavily on the edge of Calvin's bed.

Calvin crossed his arms more tightly. He didn't want that crying feeling to come back.

"Do you want to tear up this project and start another?"

"It would be like this one," said Calvin. "Only worse."

Dad spoke gently. "Calvin, think about Train."

A vision of Train, bright-eyed, glad-barking, came into Calvin's mind. He tried to push it away before it could make him feel that hollow sadness again.

"Train tried hard, didn't he?" said Dad. "He didn't give up."

Calvin thought about Train's eagerness to learn to come and sit and heel, his fast-wagging tail when Calvin praised him.

"And you kept trying," Dad continued. "You kept training him even though it took a long time. Why?"

Why? Because . . . because Train was Train. How could Calvin explain *that*? He opened his mouth and out rushed: "Because Train is a great dog. Smart and happy and interesting and . . . and big."

Dad nodded. "You saw his potential and didn't give up."

Calvin thought about Dad's words. He looked at his ugly poster. "Are you telling me to keep trying?" he said. "That I have a lot of potential?"

"Maybe." Dad smiled a little. "What do you think of that?"

"I think"—Calvin sighed—"that I am maybe tired of hearing about my potential."

"Okay," said Dad, looking startled.

"I think"—Calvin glanced at his father—"that maybe I will never see Train again."

"That could be true," said Dad.

Calvin felt that sad feeling come back to his throat. "Maybe right now," he said, "I just want to think about Train for a while."

"Okay," said Dad, rising from the bed. "We can talk later, if you want."

Calvin watched his father walk to the door, turn the knob. "Dad," he said, "Alfred Ludlott told Monk that I was good with animals, that I had a gift."

"I think he's right." Dad smiled. "It's one of your special talents."

Calvin listened to Dad's steps in the hall. He thought about Monk, with his nose always in a book. He thought about how easy it was for Monk to get good grades. Monk was a TAG. Talented and Gifted.

But he was Calvin. Calvin Hastings. C in math; C in English; C for Calvin, straight-C guy. He was no school TAG.

Then Calvin thought about Train and those

long training sessions. He and Train had worked hard. And now Train could come and sit and heel. The dog knew the meaning of "quiet."

Yeah, he, Calvin Hastings, was no school TAG. But maybe he was talented and gifted with animals. Maybe he was a dog TAG.

Dog tag.

Calvin didn't even smile at his own little joke. He looked at his lousy project. Yeah, he guessed he could do better. But right now he felt too sad and tired to try.

On Monday morning, Calvin turned in his project, his lousy project. It was a relief to get it off his hands. Each student was scheduled to give an oral presentation, and Calvin's turn was tomorrow. He wasn't sure what he would say. He didn't care. He just wanted the whole thing to be over.

That Monday, presentation followed presentation. There were masks, arrowheads, and maps. The other kids asked lots of questions. But Mexico and mimes got all mixed in Calvin's mind, and he stayed quiet the entire day.

The bus ride to Alfred Ludlott's house was quiet, too.

When Alfred Ludlott met them at his door, he grinned as Jenny and Monk zipped by for a few of his homemade brownies.

"How do you do, sir?" said Calvin.

"Fine, fine," said the poet heartily. "Better make haste and snatch a brownie before they're all gobbled down."

The rich chocolate smell tickled Calvin's nose. "No, thank you," he said.

Alfred Ludlott stared. "Calvin, are you feeling okay?"

"I am quite well, thank you, sir," said Calvin, with great politeness. "Why do you ask?"

"Because," said the poet, "you're not usually so polite."

"Yes, sir," said Calvin.

"Well, come be polite," said Alfred Ludlott, "to a new member of my household."

Calvin did not really feel like being polite. He sighed softly and dragged after the poet, who led him to the back door.

Calvin did not want to look out that door.

He did not want to see the doghouse.

It would remind him of Train.

He did not want to see the hole in the yard.

It would remind him of Train.

He especially did not want to see Fitzgerald.

Fitzgerald would remind him that Alfred Ludlott wanted a dog, but he did not want a dog named Train.

"Look," said Alfred Ludlott, pointing.

Calvin's eyes followed the poet's finger.

Calvin saw the doghouse. He saw the hole in the yard. He saw Fitzgerald prancing and wagging his tail, wagging his whole sausage body.

And, strangely enough, he saw Train.

OR WAS IT TRAIN?

Calvin had heard of mirages. He had read about folks who wanted to see something so badly that, well, they *saw* it—but as soon as they moved closer—*poof!*—it disappeared.

He didn't want to race across the yard, past the Train-dug hole and the doghouse. He didn't want to whoop and yell and reach out to hug a dog that would vanish like a Magic Squad trick.

If that happened, Calvin knew he would feel a whole lot worse than he did right now, with new hope rising, rising fast in his chest like a soft-feathered bird.

Calvin wanted to make sure that this tail-wagging, big, big dog was no mirage.

"Train," he whispered.

"Roo-roo!" an exuberant greeting rang out.

That bark was no mirage-dog bark.

"Roo-roo!"

That bark was *real*. And it was loud—*real* loud.

"Train, quiet," Calvin commanded.

Train stopped barking. He gazed expectantly at Calvin.

"Come," Calvin said.

The big dog hurtled to his side, and Calvin whispered, *"Good* dog," and scratched the lopsided ears, again and again, till at last he was completely satisfied. This dog was no mirage.

"I'll tell you what happened." Alfred Ludlott came up beside Calvin. "Yesterday Fitzgerald was looking kind of mopey, and I was feeling kind of mopey. You know that feeling of missing someone?"

Yeah, thought Calvin, I know that feeling.

"Well, seems like old Fitz and I had that feeling *bad*. I even missed a certain loud bark."

Calvin began to smile, just a little.

"See, that bark made me look outside. It reminded me there was a whole world out there, full of squirrels and flowers and trash. I had to look closer. That's good for poets."

"It is?" asked Calvin.

"Yes," said Alfred Ludlott. "To find the most descriptive words, a poet must first see things very clearly."

"And Train helped you do that?"

Alfred Ludlott nodded. "I believe," he continued, winking, "that Train is my muse."

"Ah." Calvin nodded, too. "Your muse."

"Roo," said Train, in what Calvin supposed was a muselike way.

"For some poets," Alfred Ludlott explained, "the muse is a beautiful woman or a special place. The muse is the poet's inspiration. It makes him or her want to put words on paper."

"Ah," Calvin said again. Personally, he thought Alfred Ludlott was lucky to have a fine muse like Train, rather than some boring beautiful woman or place. Who would have guessed that the humane shelter's untrained, loud-rooing dog would have blossomed into a muse?

"I'm glad," said Calvin, hoping to shift the talk away from poetry. "I'm glad you recognized Train's potential. How did you get him back from Nigel?"

The poet explained that the rescue had actually been very easy. It seemed, he told Calvin, that

Nigel did not want a dog but a fish. A small fish in a small, tidy bowl. Or perhaps—and the poet winked again—it was Nigel's *mother* who wanted the fish.

Calvin permitted himself a smile. "I told her a dog was a big responsibility."

Alfred Ludlott shook his head. "Seems all that responsibility wore her out in one day."

The poet took a deep breath, then said, "Calvin, I acted too quickly, giving Train to Nigel. I'm sorry. Nigel's home wasn't a good one for Train. Don't you think this place—with that large, well-dug hole—is much better?"

Calvin grinned then, a full-scale grin.

Train's dog grin was as big as Calvin's.

And Fitzgerald frisked with a dachshund-sized grin.

Alfred Ludlott said, "You did a great job of training this dog. It's a pleasure to welcome him home."

Before Calvin could say thanks, a cheerful "Hi!" interrupted. Dr. Jamar waved over the fence, then pointed to a delicate poodle. "Let me introduce you to Muffin, who is staying with me for a while."

Muffin. Calvin shook his head. Why do people

name their dogs after food? he wondered. And why not some *good* food like pizza?

"Are you fostering *another* dog?" he asked.

"Yup," said Dr. Jamar. "There are so many that need homes."

Calvin grew quiet. He remembered Dr. Jamar telling him that even a kid could help homeless animals. He remembered his first plans for his project. He had planned to describe the many breeds of dogs. He had planned to list the ways that kids could help.

Calvin remembered the poster he had turned in that morning.

He remembered the ragged pictures, the misspelled names, the chunks of ugly brown tape.

He had not done his best work, he knew that.

He had let Train down.

Calvin scratched Train's lopsided ears in silent apology.

"Of *course* I'm keeping Train," Alfred Ludlott was telling Dr. Jamar. "Calvin kept telling me the dog had great potential, and he was absolutely right."

"The dog of great potential," murmured Dr. Jamar.

And that was when Calvin knew he had to undo what he had done. Or at least, he had to redo it.

Never let it be said, he thought, that Calvin Hastings can be outdone by a dog.

Or can't learn from a dog like Train.

When Dad drove up to Alfred Ludlott's house that evening, Calvin pulled him aside for a quiet talk before Jenny and Monk could jump in the car.

Dad looked at his son's serious face.

"I don't know," he said finally. "I don't want all-night homework to become a habit."

Calvin shook his head.

Dad sighed. "We'll talk to Mom. I'm sure she'll have something to say."

But that night after supper, Dad did more than talk. Mom had listened to Calvin, and she had said no.

"I think," said Dad, "Calvin needs to do this."

Mom glanced at Calvin's determined face. "Okay," she said finally. "But I don't want late-hour, last-minute homework to become a habit—"

"Mom, *Mom*, okay," said Calvin. "We're wasting time. I better get started."

Mom and Dad helped him gather a stack of

magazines and lay out scissors, clear tape, and fine-tipped pens.

"Go to bed when you're finished," said Mom. "Don't stay up too late."

"We won't interrupt," said Dad. "You're on your own."

"Good," said Calvin.

The clock said 7:00.

Calvin began to work quickly and carefully. He cut new pictures slowly, slowly around the edges. This took four times longer than yesterday's chop-chop style, but it sure was neater.

The clock said 8:45.

Calvin squished down a pang of worry. He still had a lot to do.

Next, he printed short descriptions of dog breeds on white paper and glued each beside the correct dog picture. He wrote slowly, neatly. He didn't want to have to start over.

10:05.

Calvin read over his project. It was better, much better, than the one he had turned in that morning.

But he still wanted to do more.

He took another blank sheet of poster paper. He

printed the name and address of the humane shelter. He listed the number of homeless animals that died each year. He listed the ways that kids could help:

1. *Donate old towels and money to shelters.*
2. *Foster dogs and cats.*
3. *Adopt older animals rather than buying puppies, kittens, and baby rabbits at pet stores.*
4. *Have a veterinarian spay or neuter your dogs and cats if you don't think you can find good homes for all their babies.*
5. *Report abuse of animals to shelters.*
6. *Write letters to newspapers and do school reports on how to care for animals.*

Somewhere in the apartment, a shoe dropped, a light clicked, his mother's voice whispered good night.

Calvin felt he was the only person still awake in the world. For a moment, he felt big and protective, and then he felt only tired.

With blurry eyes, he read over his new poster. It was helpful, very helpful. It was full of facts.

But, Calvin decided, he wanted more than facts.

He wanted to show how these facts affected one dog. He wanted to do a poster on Train.

Well, that was more easily decided than done. Calvin glanced through all his dog magazines. There was not one dog picture that looked like Train. With his mixed-breed genes, Train was unique.

Okay, thought Calvin, I'll *draw* Train.

He heard the clock *tick-tick* on the wall, but he didn't want to look up.

It took several tries (drawing legs was quite hard), but when he had finished, Calvin was satisfied. The knobby-kneed, stick-tailed dog on the paper did look sort of like Train. Calvin had captured the lopsided ears and the lolling, pink-tongued grin.

Calvin then thought about his oral presentation. He decided he would talk about the long process of training Train. He would talk about his first glimpse of Train at the shelter, and how the large, exuberant dog made him think of a favorite song.

"Chasin' the Trane," Calvin murmured, putting his head down just for a moment.

He knew his grade would still be lowered because his project was late. He knew he could have done more research, found more pictures, maybe taken a photo of Train. He could have computer-typed a report like Jenny had. That's okay, Calvin thought. Right now, this is the best I can do.

Sometime later, Calvin heard a soft *pad-pad* sound. He opened one sleep-blurred eye.

There was Dad, yawning. Squinting at the clock. 2:45.

"Chasin' the Tr . . . ," Calvin mumbled, closing his eye again.

Calvin didn't even feel himself being lifted and guided gently down the dark hall. He didn't feel himself being tucked into bed. He didn't hear the *pad-pad-pad* of Dad's bare feet across the floor. But as he settled down, Calvin hummed and gave a loud snort.

"Humph," Dad murmured, leaving the door open a bit. "And that boy thought *I* snored."

The apartment returned to its late-night, breath-filled quiet.

And soon snores came from Mom and Dad's darkened room.

About the Author

Mary Quattlebaum received a B.A. from the College of William and Mary and an M.A. from Georgetown University. Her children's books include *Jackson Jones and the Puddle of Thorns*, *A Year on My Street*, and *Jazz, Pizzazz, and the Silver Threads*, which is the first book about Calvin Hastings and his family and friends. Mary Quattlebaum directs Arts Project Renaissance, a creative and autobiography writing program for older adults, and lives in Washington, D.C., with her husband, Christopher David, who began learning magic at eight years old and can still bake a cake in his top hat. They share their home with eight gerbils and numerous fish.

About the Illustrator

Frank Remkiewicz is the author and illustrator of more than twenty books for children and the illustrator of many more. He has also created many greeting cards, cartoons, and posters, as well as the box for a popular brand of animal crackers. He recently moved from northern California to Sarasota, Florida, with his wife and daughter.